Floppy Cat

written by:
Kari Kay

illustrations by:
Kevin Riley &
Andy Dorsett

Floppy Cat Company, Inc.
P.O. Box 91503
Sioux Falls, SD 57109

Please visit www.floppycat.com

Library of Congress Control Number: 2007906878

ISBN: 0-9768307-7-9

Author: Kari Kay
Illustrators: Kevin Riley and Andy Dorsett
Graphic Artist: Jen Pfeiffer
Developer: The Education Matters Company

Printed in the U.S.A.

08 09 10 CG 10 9 8 7 6 5 4 3 2 1

See how many times you can find
me throughout the book!

Thanks to those who saw the Floppy Cat in me.

Floppy cat taught me so many life lessons. The most important of which, is that we all deal with challenges. We can choose to run from those challenges and play it safe, or we can boldly step into them to learn and grow. Floppy lived his life with a positive, never give up attitude, always looking for the good in every situation. My hope is that after reading this book, you and your child will find the Floppy Cat inside of you!

Kari Kay

Floppy was an unusual cat,

He could always be seen swaying
this way and that.

His sisters and brothers would all run, jump, and play,
while Floppy would flip and flop, flop in the hay.

Even though he had trouble keeping up with the pace,
he could always be seen with a smile on his face.

One day he sat watching the
others play ball.

Wondering how it would be if
he did not have to fall.

He asked his mother, "Why is it that I always flip, flop and sway, why don't I move in a more 'cat-like' way?"

"All cats are unique in their own special way. You just happen to flip, flop, and sway."

"Oh Floppy," said his mother, as she gave him a kiss, "Your floppiness is your own special gift."

From that day on, his floppiness
was less a concern.

He always moved forward and
was willing to learn.

He spent his days flipping and flopping around.
The big red barn was his giant playground!

He knew that red barn like the back of his paw.
Every nook, every cranny, the scent of the straw.

One day Floppy noticed something he'd never seen before.
A red piece of cloth stuck in the rickety floor.

What could it be? He was curious to see.
"That red piece of cloth is puzzling me!"

Floppy flipped and flopped
as fast as he could.

Down the bales, through the stall and
over the big pile of wood.

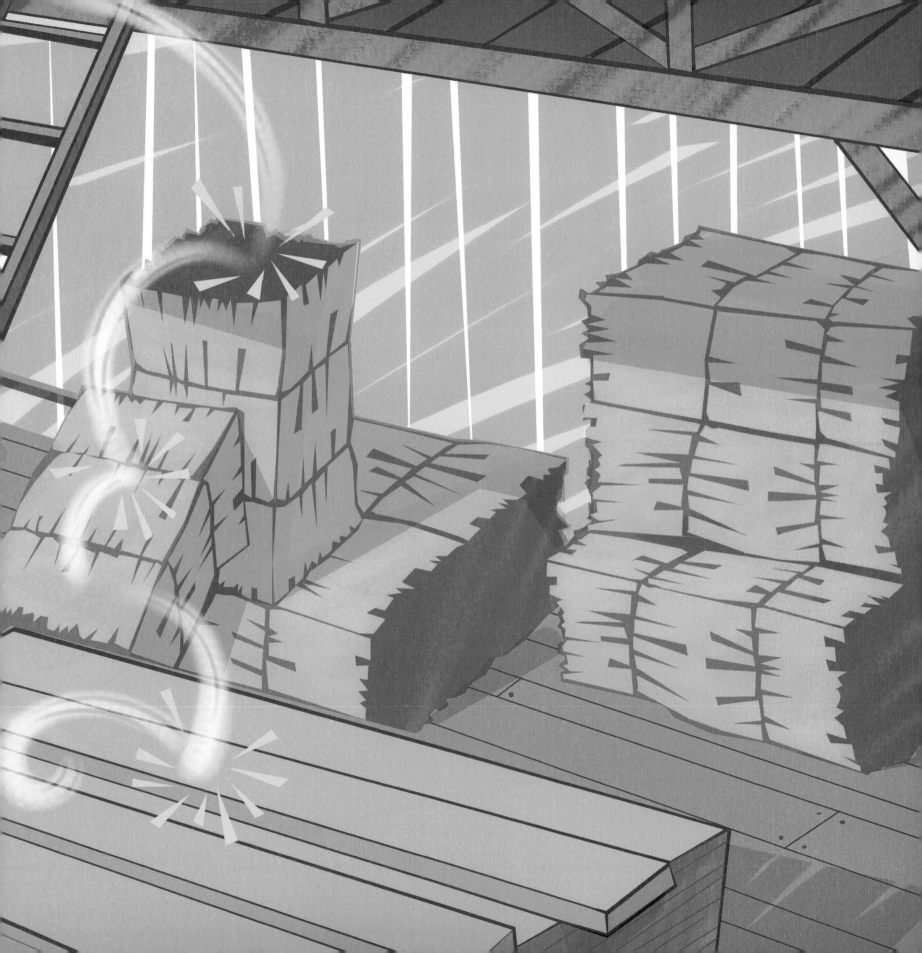

As he reached the red cloth
he was all out of breath.

His eyes wide with hope,
his hair was a mess!

He grabbed the red cloth
and pulled with all his might.

When suddenly it came loose
and sent him flying out of sight!

Floppy landed on top of
a tall stack of hay,
he brushed himself off and
hoped his tail was ok.

Then he looked and he looked and he looked all around,
Wondering where that mysterious red cloth could be found.

"Look on your head," his friends laughed from below.
"Can you do that again? That was an excellent show!"

So Floppy looked over his shoulder
and saw his dusty reflection.

There it was, a red hat,
sitting in a silly direction.

The cap was soft and bright red in its color.

The likes of which he had seen no other.

He examined it closely both inside and out,

curious to see what the hat was about.

Inside the cap, he found
a note that was hidden.

Special instructions for use
that someone had written.

So he put on the cap
and hurried out the door,

something he hadn't
thought much of doing before.

His new found confidence put
a spring in his stride,

bounding through the tall grass,
wearing his hat with great pride!

He sang to himself as he skipped right along,
a cheerfull, upbeat and carefree song!

I can be whatever I want to be,
as long as I always believe in me!

He decided to rest under the big maple tree,
where he dreamed of all he would do, be, and see.

Happy and content he watched the sunset,
THIS WAS A DAY HE WOULD NEVER FORGET!

Floppy would love to hear your
stories, dreams and goals.

WWW.FLOPPYCAT.COM